The Things I **Love** About
Playtime

Trace Moroney

The Five Mile Press

I **love** playtime,
and these are things
I love most . . .

climbing trees

making things out
of play-dough

and *trying* to do
magic tricks.

abracadabra!

I **especially** love playing dress-ups!
I can pretend to be
anything I want . . .

like a ferocious dragon

or, a king that rules the world

or, a magical fairy that can
make wishes come true!

I have lots of fun playing on my own –
but, I **really** love to play
with my friends.

We like to play at the park where
there are lots of things to do.

And, we love to play in the snow
until our cheeks turn bright pink
and our noses turn blue!

But, our favourite thing to play together
is hide-and-seek . . . in the dark!

I find someone hiding by shining my
torchlight on them . . . then I shout
"Bunny-Boo! I found you!"
We laugh and laugh
and laugh.

I love playing with my family too.

Dad pretends to be a growly tiger
and chases me and tickles me
until I squeal with laughter.

We go on bike rides together.

And, sometimes, we play board games
or card games together.

Playtime with Mum and Dad
is so much fun . . . we laugh
and giggle a lot.

Playing by myself,
or with my friends, or
with my family makes me
feel special and safe
and happy and
loved.

I **love** playtime!

Notes for Parents and Caregivers

'The Things I Love' series shares simple examples of creating **positive thinking** about everyday situations our children experience.

A positive attitude is simply the inclination to generally be in an optimistic, hopeful state of mind. Thinking positively is not about being unrealistic. Positive thinkers recognise that bad things can happen to pessimists and optimists alike – however, it is the positive thinkers who *choose* to focus on the hope and opportunity available within every situation.

Researchers of positive psychology have found that people with positive attitudes are more creative, tolerant, generous, constructive, successful and open to new ideas and new experiences than those with a negative attitude. Positive thinkers are happier, healthier, live longer, experience more satisfying relationships, and have a greater capacity for love and joy.

I have used the word **love** numerous times throughout each book, as I think it best describes the *feeling* of living in an optimistic and hopeful state of mind, and it is a simple but powerful word that is used to emphasise our positive thoughts about people, things, situations and experiences.

Playtime

Play provides a fun and secure forum in which children acquire and build social expertise. They learn how to negotiate, cooperate, form friendships and resolve conflicts. The benefits of play include the promotion of imagination, increased confidence, growth of language and communication, an enhanced sense of control, and an opportunity for self-expression.

As well as alleviating anxiety, play provides an opportunity to try out new ways of thinking and problem-solving, and to overcome physical and mental challenges. Play also promotes physical development by building balance, strength, coordination and fine motor skills.

Play, or playfulness, encourages as all to laugh more, which in itself has massive health benefits … and is extremely contagious!

Trace Moroney

For my dog Poppy, while ageing gracefully —
has never forgotten how to be playful . . .
a great reminder for me to be the same!

Dare to Love

The Five Mile Press Pty Ltd
1 Centre Road, Scoresby
Victoria 3179 Australia
www.fivemile.com.au
Illustrations and text copyright © Trace Moroney, 2009
All rights reserved
www.tracemoroney.com
First published 2009
Printed in China 10 9 8 7 6 5
National Library of Australia Cataloguing-in-Publication entry
Moroney, Trace
The things I love about playtime / Trace Moroney.
1st ed.
9781742116594 (hbk.)
9781742116808 (pbk.)
For pre-school age.
Play--Juvenile literature.
158.1